Set 5

TITLE I
Vincennes Community School Corp.

To my mother, Nellie Bullock Franklin

ABBY

by Jeannette Franklin Caines

pictures by Steven Kellogg

HarperCollins*Publishers*

Library of Congress Catalog Card Number: 73-5480
ISBN 0-06-020921-6
ISBN 0-06-020922-4 (lib. bdg.)
ISBN 0-06-443049-9 (pbk.)

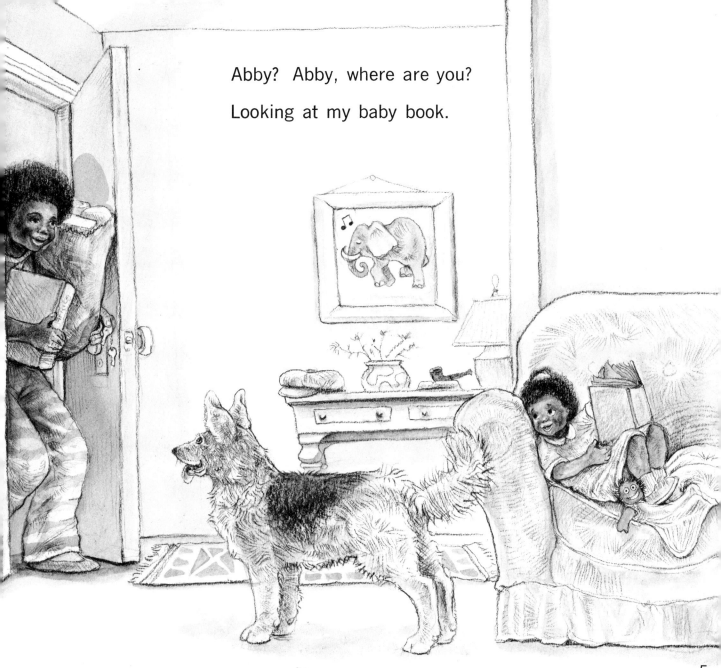

Abby? Abby, where are you?

Looking at my baby book.

5

Ma, where did I come from?

Manhattan.

How old was I when you and Daddy got me?

Eleven months and thirteen days.

What did I have on?

The pink dress you have on your doll now,
white shoes, and a blue coat with a hood.

Come, Abby, lunch time
and Kevin will be here in no time flat.

Can I bring my book?

If you don't get any food on it.

9

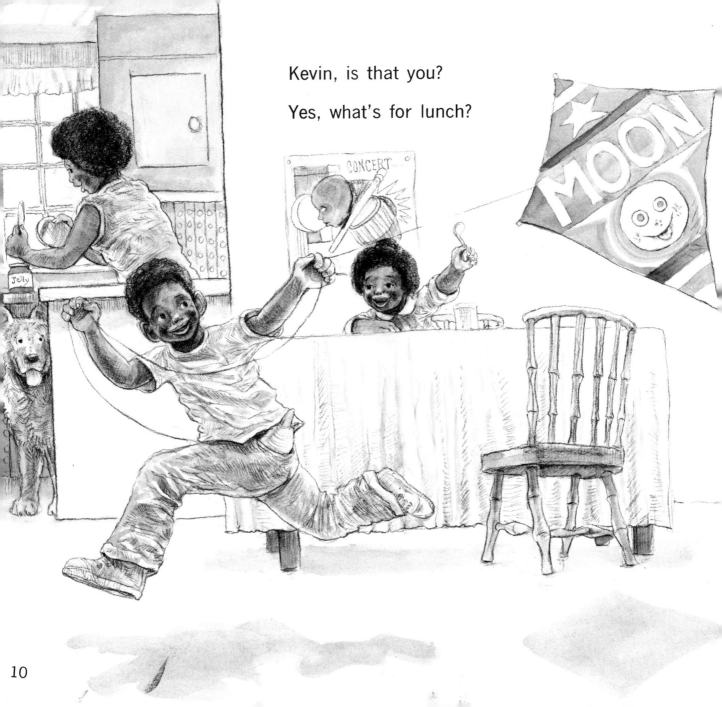

Kevin, is that you?

Yes, what's for lunch?

10

Kevin, you want to look at my baby pictures?

No, I don't have time.

Kevin, what did you say when you first saw me?

Oh, Abby! I don't know.

12

Yes you do. Here it is and you can read it to me.

I don't have time.

I will read it. Kevin said, "Ugh, a girl."

Don't you like girls?

No, no, no!

14

15

I'm a boy, Kevin.

No, you're a girl. I'm a boy.

16

No, you're a girl.

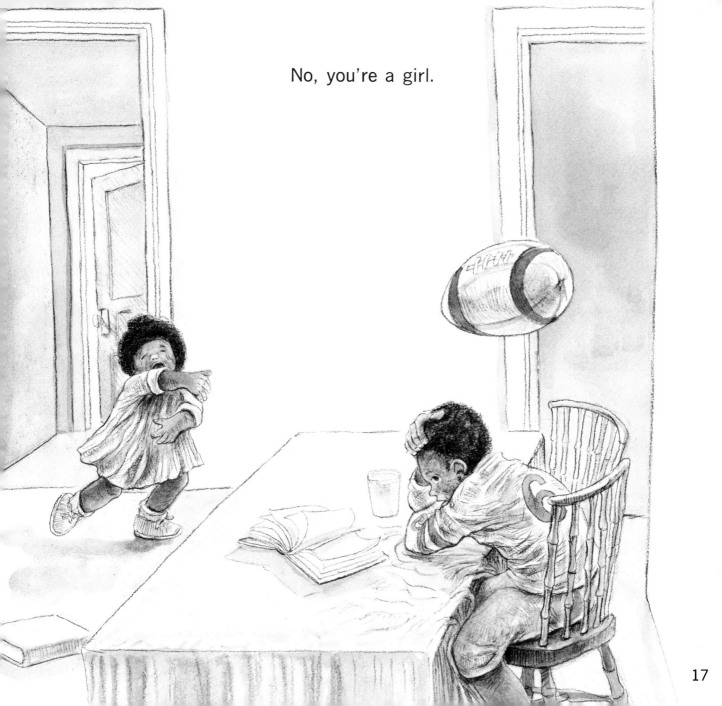

Why she always gotta cry like that?

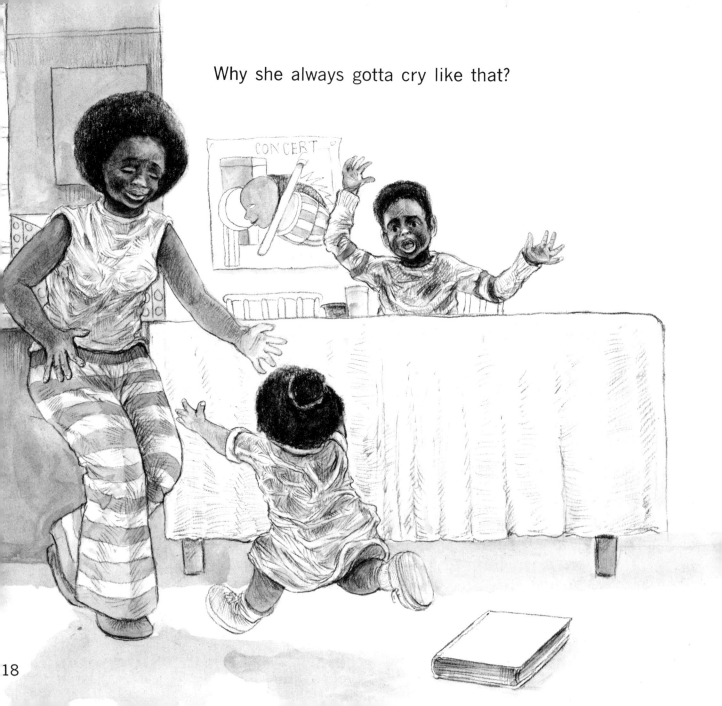

Kevin, Abby loves you
and she thinks you don't like her because she's a girl.

Okay, girl, I like you.

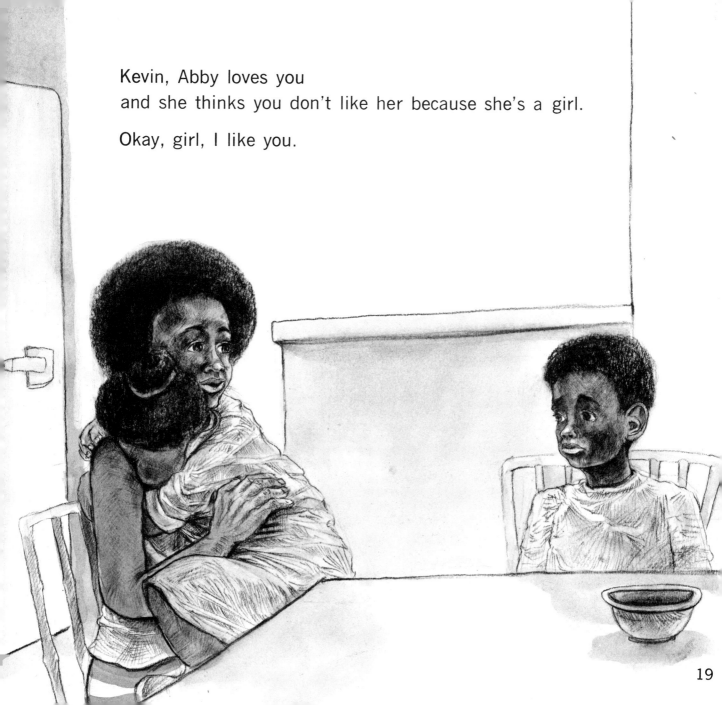

I'm a g-i-r-l !

Okay, okay, I'll read one page.

YOUR FIRST VISITORS.

I know, I know—Grandma Nellie.

YOUR FIRST WORDS.

Bottle.

Ma, can I bring Abby for show-and-tell next week? Miss Paige said it's okay.

What are you going to tell about me?

That you're adopted, that we get to keep you forever, and I gave you my fire engine for your birthday. Ma, can I?

We'll see.

24

I'm going now.

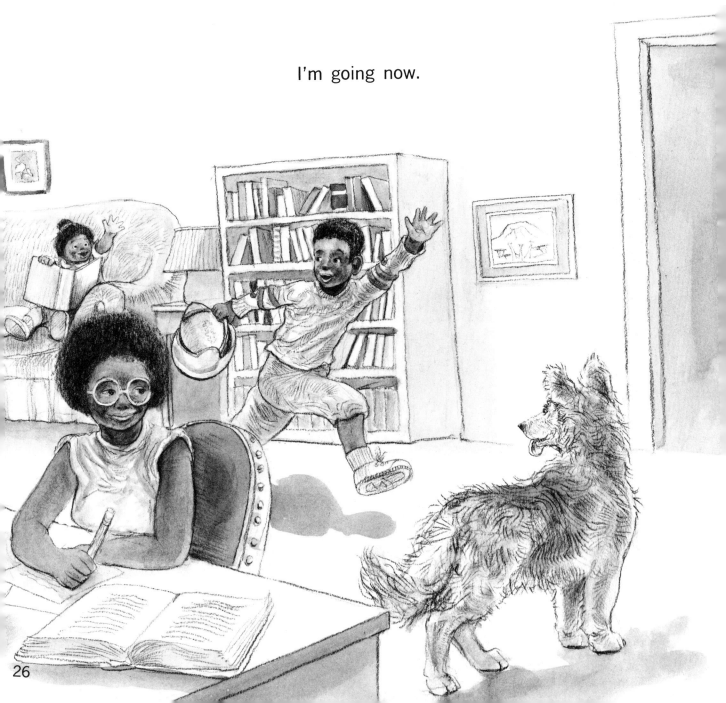

Kevin, will you bring me a surprise?

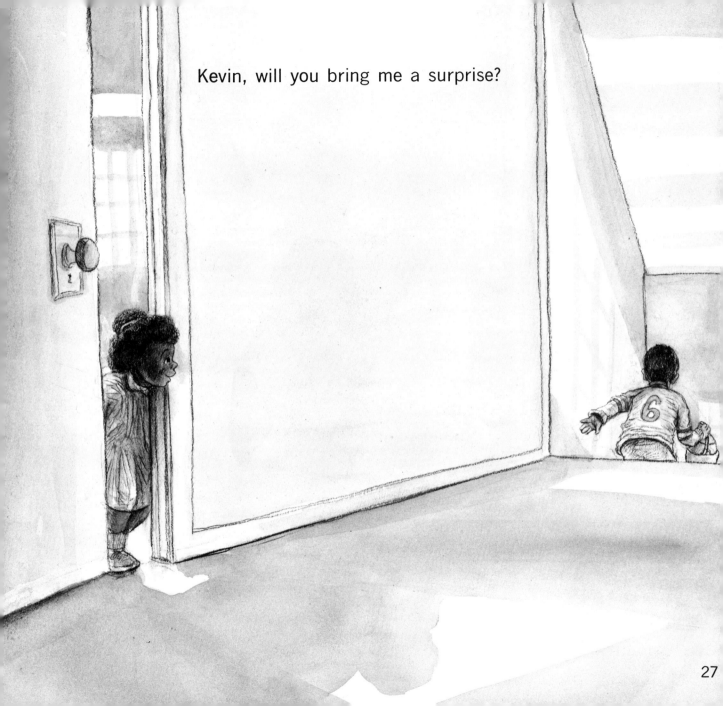

27

If you find my turtle stamp.

Was Kevin adopted too?

No.

Let's adopt a boy for Kevin
and I'll save my crib and pillow for him.

We'll talk about it with Daddy
when he comes home tonight.